SOCCER SENSATION

WITHDRAWN
PUBLIC LIBRARY
BROOKLINE

BY JAKE MADDOX

Text by Sigmund Brouwer
Illustrated by Katie Wood

STONE ARCH BOOKS
a capstone imprint

Jake Maddox is published by Stone Arch Books, an imprint of Capstone.
1710 Roe Crest Drive
North Mankato, Minnesota 56003
www.capstonepub.com

Library of Congress Cataloging-in-Publication Data is available on the Library of Congress website.

ISBN: 978-1-4965-9703-8 (library binding)
ISBN: 978-1-4965-9919-3 (paperback)
ISBN: 978-1-4965-9754-0 (eBook PDF)

Summary: Cameron Jones plays soccer not because he loves it, but because his dad believes that one day the game will help him earn a college scholarship. When his father's job transfer takes him from the big city to a small-town team, Cameron thinks it might be his chance to take a step back from soccer.

Designer: Elyse White

Printed and bound in the USA.
PA117

TABLE OF CONTENTS

CHAPTER 1

BAD NEWS

Cameron Jones stood behind the sideline at midfield. The referee handed him the soccer ball to throw in toward the awaiting players. Three minutes remained in the game. Cameron's team—the Royal Blues—were up 3–2 against the Cardinals. A win today would guarantee his team first place in the league.

With the ball held firmly with both hands above his head, Cameron scanned the field. The Royals wore blue jerseys. The Cardinals wore red.

Careful, Cameron told himself above the crowd noise. *Careful*.

At least 200 people were watching the game from the stands. This was the premier league for Cameron's age level, which consisted mostly of eighth graders.

The stars of this league had bright futures. The best players were just a few years away from being fast-tracked to programs that led to college scholarships.

That's why he and his father spent at least half an hour each night on soccer drills, no matter what the weather was like. If it rained too hard, his father would move the cars out of the garage and make room for Cameron to practice there instead.

In the end, it would pay off in a college scholarship. At least that's what his father hoped.

As Cameron looked for an open Royal, his father's voice echoed in his head. *Don't try to do too much. Under pressure, it's too easy to make a mistake. Play the odds. Play it safe.*

As if his father could read his mind, Cameron heard a familiar voice coming from the stands. "Smart choice, Cam!" his dad called out. "You can do it. Smart choice!"

Cameron knew what that meant.

Smart choices are easier to make than great plays. At least that's what his dad always said. Make the smartest choice every time you have the ball. This will get you a college scholarship. Smart choices mattered.

It's why Cameron was on the Royal Blues. The coach was known for guiding players into making smart choices. They also had the best discipline and knew how to play as a team.

Trouble was, Cameron was finding it hard to care. Soccer wasn't fun anymore. It wasn't like it used to be. The excitement was gone. Now it was just about making smart choices. But what did it matter if he no longer really wanted to play? Quitting was not an option.

Refocusing on the game, Cameron took a deep breath. He reminded himself to keep both feet on the ground as he threw the ball.

Another piece of his father's advice played in his mind. *Do it again and again so that it becomes routine in practice, because there is no such thing as routine in a pressure situation.*

Cameron looked for an open blue player. It wasn't easy. The Cardinals clogged the middle of the field. This took away a direct attack. Other opposing players danced around the edges. They stuck close to Cameron's teammates and took away any easy target.

He faked a throw one way. Then he saw his teammate, Steve Martindale, break loose on the other side of the field.

Steve stopped. He dashed forward, faked a move to the left. He then spun back. Steve was wide open. It would be a long throw, but it was doable. And it would set Steve up for a good attack on the net.

But . . .

They were up by a goal, with just a few minutes remaining in the game. All they needed to do was hold on to the ball until the final whistle.

Cameron faked the throw again toward Steve, and then launched the ball into the back field, where another teammate was wide open.

It was an easy play. It was also the smart choice.

The Royal Blues ran down the clock, guaranteeing first place.

That was the good news for Cameron, but he still didn't feel very excited about the safe win.

Soon after the game ended, his father met him in the parking lot.

"Well played, Cam," his father, James Jones, said. He still wore his suit from the office.

They walked toward the car. His father paused and put a hand on Cameron's shoulder. "Well, buddy, I wish I didn't have to deliver this news after such a great game, but I've been transferred at work. We have to move to a small town named Evansville."

"What? Evansville?" Cameron stared at his father in confusion. "Where's Evansville?"

CHAPTER 2

WHERE'S THE COACH?

Two weeks later, Cameron stood alone along the sideline of the soccer field. It was Saturday morning, and he waited for practice to start with his new team. Practice was supposed to begin ten minutes ago, but there was no sign of the coach.

He was not impressed by what he saw as a handful of boys began to gather on the field. To Cameron, they looked nothing like any soccer team he played with before.

First off, nobody wore shirts that matched their shorts. In fact, none of their shirts or shorts even matched what any of the other players wore. Cameron's old team had special practice uniforms. Here, it was like each player had just rolled out of bed and grabbed whatever they could find on the floor to wear.

Second, there were no cones set up on the field for passing and shooting drills.

Third, nobody was there to take the lead and organize the practice.

Still no sign of the coach! Cameron thought. The growing group of players just stood around in small groups, laughing and joking. A few players were kicking around soccer balls.

Back in the city where he played all his life, many teams needed to use the soccer field. Nobody would waste time like this during the few hours given for a practice session.

Cameron told himself not to be surprised. It seemed that Evansville barely had more than two traffic lights. He should not expect much from the only team in the area that was in his age group. Especially after he and his father searched online to see if the coach and team were any good. They found out that the coach's name was Kelly Harrison, but except for a game schedule, there were no search results for "Kelly Harrison + soccer + Evansville."

There was, however, a bright side to this. For the last year, he had been waiting for the right opportunity to quit soccer. Playing had stopped being fun. A team this bad would give him a good excuse. A safe exit that his father would hopefully accept.

As this thought crossed his mind, Cameron couldn't help feeling guilty. He looked out at the stands and saw his father. His dad would be so disappointed in him if he quit soccer.

He was also surprised that with the exception of his father, the stands were empty. Back in the city, even for a practice, the stands would be filled with parents.

Cameron turned back to face the field and saw a player walking toward him. He was tall and skinny and his blond hair stuck out in all directions. "Hey, I'm Drew Allen. You're the new guy. Cameron, right? Coach told us to expect you. Welcome to the Blazers."

"Thanks," Cameron said. "Um, where's Mr. Harrison?"

"*Mr.* Harrison? Our coach is not a mister," Drew answered with a chuckle.

Cameron was confused. Maybe this was the wrong team. No. Drew and the other players were expecting him. Still—

"Coach Kelly Harrison," Cameron said, almost asking as a question. "Over the phone, his wife told us just to show up."

She hadn't even asked if Cameron had skills. She'd just said Cameron would be welcome to join the team. How good could the Blazers be if you didn't need to try out for the team?

Drew laughed. "Coach Kelly is a woman. You were probably talking to her! Easy to get confused, I guess, with a name that could belong to a male or female."

She? They had a woman coach? Cameron knew his dad preferred male coaches because he thought they were better at controlling players.

"Oh," Cameron said, trying to get over the fact that his coach was a woman. "Well . . . Where is she?"

"She just got married and spends most Saturday mornings helping her husband run his home business," Drew said. "She gets here when she gets here. Don't worry though. She always shows up."

This did not sound like a coach who cared much about molding a team, Cameron thought.

Drew pointed past Cameron. "She's here now!"

Cameron looked over his shoulder. Coach Kelly wore a silver and white tracksuit. She was medium height, with short blond hair and a big grin.

"Hey everybody!" she shouted. "It's shoe time! No drills this morning."

"Shoe time?" Cameron asked Drew.

Drew was already bent over, pulling off one of his shoes.

"Yeah." He stood up holding the shoe. "We're about to split into teams. We toss shoes into a pile and then divide the pile. Half will be wearing shirts. The other half plays without shirts. Makes it way easier to know who is on your team for our scrimmage."

Two sets of jerseys would do the same thing, Cameron thought. But he didn't say anything as he bent over and untied his shoe.

He hoped he would be playing on the shirts team. The only part of his upper body that was tanned was his arms, and he didn't want anyone to laugh at how pale everything else was.

CHAPTER 3

YOU'LL THANK ME LATER

"Right there!" His dad jumped off the couch and pointed at the television screen. He hit the pause button on the remote.

"Who is out of position?" he excitedly asked.

Cameron and his dad were watching a World Cup game from a few years ago. France versus England. A midfielder had just passed the ball to a fellow teammate.

Cameron scanned the screen. The camera had panned back, showing most of the field.

"That midfielder for England," Cameron said. "France has the ball. He should be marking his man. But he's at least three steps away."

Marking his man. To his friends, Cameron might have said "guarding," not "marking." But his dad liked to be exact when it came to soccer, and that was the term used.

"Well done," said Dad. "Now keep watching."

Cameron's dad hit reverse and paused again. "See that pass? Intercepted. Why?"

Cameron had seen dozens of similar situations on the television. This is part of why it seemed like playing soccer was work, not fun. "The winger tried to be a hero. Long pass. If he makes it, the other winger gets to break loose. But he had a one in ten chance of making it."

"Maybe one in fifteen," Dad countered.

Cameron bit back his frustration. It seemed as if he never had the "right enough" answer for his dad. Did it make a difference whether it was one in ten or one in fifteen? Either way, any attempt by the player to go for the long shot was a risk not worth taking.

"Scan the field again. Which was the safer pass?" Dad asked.

That was obvious to Cameron. "Behind and to the right. Then the winger could have gone wide and forced the defenders to open up the field."

He heard applause behind him. Cameron grinned as he turned and looked at his mom who had just walked into the room. She was tall with shoulder-length brunette hair. She always seemed to be smiling.

"He's got this figured out, James," she said. "Maybe you boys can help unpack now?"

"Give us ten more minutes, Honey," James answered. "You'll thank me when our son gets a scholarship."

"Ten minutes and not a second more," Cameron's mom said as she turned and left the room.

"Dad, about this scholarship stuff," Cameron said as he faced his father. "I need to tell you something."

Maybe this would be the best time to tell his dad that he wasn't sure if he wanted to work this hard at soccer. Especially since it looked like this small-town soccer program wasn't that good.

"No need to thank me yet," his dad grinned. "Lots of work to do still."

Cameron loved his dad and hated the thought of disappointing him. He decided to wait for a better time to tell him he wanted to quit. He swallowed a sigh and said, "You bet."

His dad advanced the frames on the television and stopped again. "Look at what happens because the midfielder got caught out of position when the ball was intercepted by France. His fault?"

Before Cameron could reply, his father answered. "Of course it was his fault. He should have played it safe. His pass didn't work out. Keep watching this play out."

With the midfielder unable to stay with his man, France had a six on four advantage. Six attackers against four defenders. Moments later France scored. Game over.

His dad shut off the television and settled back in the couch. "I've been thinking about what you said about today's practice. Especially how undisciplined the team is."

"You were there," said Cameron. "The coach was twenty minutes late. All we did was play a scrimmage the entire time. No drills. No practice of individual skills."

"I've made it clear I had no choice but to take the job transfer, right?" his dad continued.

Cameron nodded his head.

"So I can't help the fact that you are playing on a low-grade team in the middle of nowhere. But I can help with the discipline. We need this team to succeed so that scouts will take notice. So I plan on talking to your coach and volunteer to help."

"Well . . . ," Cameron hesitated.

"Don't thank me until you get your college scholarship." His dad chuckled again. "Right?"

"Yeah," Cameron said. He tried to show enthusiasm. His dad wanted so badly for Cameron to be a star. "Right."

"Great then," his dad said as he got up from the couch. "Now let's help Mom."

CHAPTER 4

BIG CITY ATTITUDE?

"Cam, buddy! Go get 'em!"

It was his dad's voice coming from the spectator stands behind him.

Cameron was tying his shoe as the players got ready for the game to begin. Once done, he stood up and turned around to face the crowd.

He saw his father giving him the thumbs-up sign. Cameron gave him one in return. He wasn't sure if he felt it, though.

He knew his father would be recording the match and commenting later on every choice Cameron made during the game.

Cameron turned back to the field.

"Hey, Cameron!" Drew yelled from midfield. "Ready?"

Cameron trotted onto the field for their game against the Chargers. And just like that, his team's orange jerseys and the Chargers' purple jerseys were in motion.

***

Five minutes left in the game, and the score was tied at two. This game wasn't a do-or-die event for Cameron's team. The Blazers only needed to win one of their last three games to make the playoffs. Still, it would be great to win today and be assured a place in the championship games.

Cameron moved toward the other goal and sprinted for an open spot. He was clear!

Blazers had the ball. Kyle Fenton dribbled toward a maze of players. He was the fastest runner on the team, and Cameron had been impressed by Kyle's ball handling abilities.

"Open," Cameron called out.

Kyle glanced up. There was an easy alley to advance the ball to Cameron. Kyle faked a pass, but he held on to the ball. He tried to make a move to beat the defender but lost the ball.

The Chargers took over. Ten seconds later they scored a goal to lead by one.

Cameron ran beside Kyle.

"You didn't see me?" Cameron asked, annoyed.

"Win some, lose some," Kyle answered. "Never know what's going to work until you try it."

"I was open," Cameron said, growing more frustrated. "It was the smart play."

"Don't sweat it, Big City," said Kyle.

Big City? Cameron was surprised at Kyle's tone of voice. Calling Cameron "Big City" came across as rude, as if Kyle was mad that Cameron had pointed out the smart play.

"Just trying to help the team," Cameron said.

"How about you just relax then?" Kyle answered as he moved away. "We're here to have fun. And there's still plenty of time left in the game."

Cameron decided to focus on the ball instead of his feelings. The only good thing was that his dad would agree that Cameron had made the smart choice.

About a minute later, his focus paid off when the ball popped loose in his direction.

Cameron gathered it in, dribbled the ball, and moved slowly up the field, looking for an open man.

There it was—an orange-shirt Blazer, with nobody from the other team covering. All that was needed was a short, easy pass. He soon realized the open player was Kyle.

Cameron was tempted to hang on to the ball. But it was more important to make a smart choice. *Set emotions aside,* he told himself. *Make the smart choice.*

Cameron could picture the play. Make a short, safe pass to advance the ball then get open for a return pass. He gave the ball a firm tap. It was a perfect pass.

Cameron sprinted hard and found the opening. All Kyle needed to do was get him the ball and they'd have a good scoring chance.

"Here!" Cameron shouted. "Here! I'm open!"

Kyle glanced at him again, held on to the ball, and tried to beat two defenders by going between them.

No surprise. Bad choice. Bad result. The Chargers took control of the ball. A minute later, the game ended with the Blazers on the losing end.

Cameron sighed.

If this continued, he was going to hate soccer even more than he already did.

CHAPTER 5

COACH NEEDS HELP

"The team showed no discipline," Dad said to Cameron. They were standing on the sidelines as most of the players left with their parents. "You should have never lost the game. Don't you agree?"

Cameron nodded. When his dad was in a bad mood, it was smart to just agree.

"And your coach definitely needs help, right?" Dad continued.

Cameron nodded again.

"Follow me," his dad said, as he headed toward the parking lot.

Coach Kelly had the trunk to her car open when they reached her. She lifted her gear bag and set it inside. When she turned and saw them, she smiled at Cameron.

"Hey," she said. "Good game. You gave it a hundred percent today. We can't ask for much more than that. Great job, Cameron."

She smiled at his dad. "You should be proud of him."

"I spend a lot of time helping him understand the game," James Jones said. "When it comes to soccer, rule number one in our house is making the smart choice. Glad it showed for Cameron out there today."

"We lost this one, but more often than not we win," Coach Kelly said, looking up at Cameron's father. "What I love is when the kids are giving it their best and having fun. It's amazing how quickly their skills improve when you give them space to make mistakes."

"Never hurts to help them understand game strategy though," James said.

"True enough, but—" Coach started.

"Glad we're on the same page," James said, interrupting Coach Kelly. "I've done some coaching myself."

"Nice!" Coach Kelly shut her trunk.

"And I heard from one of the moms that you'll be gone for a week or so to help your husband with his business," James continued.

"It's a start-up," Coach Kelly said. "We're having fun building it from scratch. The team is in a solid position, and they can still meet without me. They'll just scrimmage. Keeps them in shape and they have fun."

"Well, I'd be happy to help as an assistant coach until you're back," Dad said. "I'm pretty good at running practices. I have some great drills. I've also been certified by the National Soccer Association, so you can trust me."

Coach Kelly didn't take long to think about it. "Sure. It never hurts for the players to get a different perspective on the game. It would be great if you spend about half of the practice letting them kick the ball around for fun. One of my foundations is that I encourage creativity too. I'm okay if they make mistakes because they can learn from it. Sound good?"

"Sounds more than good," James said. He shook hands with Coach Kelly. "Thanks. I think you'll like what you'll see when you get back. By the way, my name is James. I guess you can call me Coach James now."

CHAPTER 6

PYLONS AND DRILLS

When the whistle blew at the next practice, players turned around and stared in surprise. It was as if they had never heard a whistle before.

"Come on in and listen up!" James's voice carried clearly across the field. He waved for the players to join him by the sidelines where he'd set up a whiteboard on an easel.

"Go ahead and sit," he said, as they slowly started to gather around. "Get comfortable. This might take a while."

Cameron noticed the players giving each other looks of surprise. A few of them shrugged. Eventually, all of them sat down.

"Coach Kelly is gone for the week," James started addressing the players, "and she's asked me to take over while she's away. My name is James Jones, and I'm Cameron's father. I'd prefer if you called me Mr. Jones, or even better, Coach Jones. I've been involved in coaching soccer for years. I thought I'd start by asking Cameron to pass along one of my favorite sayings. Cameron?"

Cameron had heard it more times than he could count. Now all eyes were on him, and it didn't feel good. "Alone, you can travel fast," Cameron tried to say as confidently as he could, "but together, you can travel far."

"Thanks, Cameron," Coach Jones said, as he turned back and stared at the blank faces of the other players. "The saying makes sense, right?"

Nobody answered.

Coach Jones continued. "Let me explain then. All of you are great players as individuals. You should be proud of yourselves. But if we work together and make smart choices, we can be even better as a team. Does that make sense?"

When nobody answered, Coach Jones pointed to Kyle. "Make sense?"

Cameron knew his Dad was asking Kyle because Kyle's mistake had cost them the game-losing goal against the Chargers.

Kyle waited a few seconds before he answered. "Sure."

"Good," Coach Jones said. "So you should like what I've drawn up here."

He pointed at the easel and continued his lesson. "This is from the last game, just before the Chargers scored on us in the final minute and won the game."

He moved his finger over the drawing. "All the Os are you guys. All the Xs are the opposing team. You can see I've already drawn each player in position, about thirty seconds before the Chargers scored."

Coach Jones looked at Kyle again, then pointed at an O. "This is where you were, Kyle. You can see that you're just short of midfield. You had possession of the ball at the time."

Kyle raised his hand.

"Yes?" Coach Jones said.

"I'm just curious as to how you know this," Kyle asked.

"I like to record the games and analyze them later," Coach Jones explained.

"That's a lot of work," Kyle remarked.

"Thanks," Coach Jones said.

Unlike his dad, Cameron wasn't sure Kyle had meant that as a compliment.

"Now Kyle," Coach Jones said, "don't take this wrong. But you tried to get past the X in front of you and lost the ball."

Moving his hands quickly, Coach Jones pointed at one X, then another X, and then a third. "See how they are spread apart on the field like this? Turning the ball over to them put these players at a disadvantage. They couldn't get back into play soon enough, because they were charging up the field."

Coach Jones pointed at one O, then another, then a third.

"On the other hand, Kyle, just before you lost the ball, you could have kicked a short pass straight sideways here," Coach Jones pointed at another O. "If you did that—made the smart choice—we would have kept possession. You know why?"

Kyle didn't respond, so Coach Jones continued talking.

"The other players would not have been caught in a bad place," he said. "Then you could have gone toward the sideline upfield. This would have drawn a defender to open up the middle and make it easy to advance the ball. Understood?"

Nobody replied.

"No problem," Coach Jones said. "I've got some pylons. We're going to set them up where the Xs were. Then each of you will take your positions. We'll run the play over again. This time, Kyle, let's see what happens when you make the smart choice and the short pass. I promise all of you will understand it much better when we practice it a few times."

Coach Jones blew the whistle and pointed to the field. "Let's move!"

CHAPTER 7

NOT A SMART CHOICE

The next afternoon, the Blazers were playing against the Volts. Coach Kelly had planned on rescheduling the game. Thanks to Cameron's dad volunteering to help while she was away, the game was now on.

Crossing midfield with the ball, Cameron saw the number 8 on the back of José Padilla's jersey. José was medium build, with dark hair and quick feet. It was a smart choice to choose him as a target. Cameron made the short pass. José trapped it perfectly.

A Volts player moved to cover Cameron and take away a return pass up the field.

Cameron drifted backward.

The Volts player faded away. It was clear they were spreading out for zone coverage. This meant choosing an area of the field to protect, instead of sticking with individual players to guard.

That gave Cameron a chance to be open again. It wouldn't help them advance the ball, but he was a safety outlet if José needed help. This was something that the team had practiced last week during the drills set up by his father.

Seconds later, José did need that help. Two Volts players moved in, one from each side. They were pinching away any safe pass that José could make up the field.

But this drew them out of position, no longer guarding other players.

As if he was sitting in front of the television with his dad holding the remote and freezing the image, Cameron could picture the field like it was a chessboard. Up along the right side of the field, two Blazers—Drew Allen and Kyle Fenton—were wide open.

Both were also quick players and great at ball handling. Get them the ball and the two of them would push their way into the attack zone and have a great scoring opportunity.

It appeared to Cameron that José saw it too. Volts players were too close to him. But any pass in their direction would be almost certainly intercepted by the incoming Volts.

Come on, Cameron thought. *Do the right thing.*

All José needed to do was pass the ball back to Cameron, who would have the perfect angle to redirect the ball to Drew. In an instant, the trap set by the two Volts players would snap shut on nothing.

"Here!" Cameron called out, though he felt that he should not have needed to say that. They had done this drill endlessly in practice to rehearse for exactly this situation.

José dribbled forward a few more steps, then faked a pass up the field and tried to beat his closest opponent by going around him. If he managed to break loose, it would give the Blazers a great scoring opportunity.

It might have worked, but José lost control of the ball. It was just enough for the Volts player to slide into the ball and kick it to his teammate.

That gave them both a straight arrow down the field. Cameron was too far over to intercept them.

He had no choice but to give chase as the other team moved closer toward the Blazers' net.

Thirty seconds later, the Volts had scored.

Thirty seconds after that, José was standing on the sidelines, replaced by the substitute sent in by Cameron's dad.

CHAPTER 8

COACH WHO?

Forty minutes later, Cameron and his dad sat at a corner table in a coffee shop with José Padilla and his father. José's father introduced himself as Michael. Michael had dark hair and was going bald. He was tall with a heavy build and wore glasses with a thick frame.

Two untouched cups of coffee rested on the table in front of both men. Cameron and José were each working on two glasses of chocolate milk. José sat across from Cameron, but kept looking past his teammate, as if the opposite wall was interesting.

Michael smiled and spoke to Cameron's father. "Thanks for meeting," he said. "You might think I wanted to talk about your choice to pull José from the game. But that's not the reason I wanted to meet."

José chimed in. "I messed up. I deserved to be pulled from the game. Especially after all the drills we did for that exact situation. I'm sorry about that."

"You're in charge when Coach Kelly isn't here," Michael added. "So we trust the reason for your decision, and we've learned the lesson."

"That part is never fun for a coach," Cameron's dad said. "When Cameron was younger, he'd hold on to the ball all the time. After they pulled him a few times, he finally began to play with discipline. It's why his other team was so successful. It's about winning. But it's also about setting them up for the future. You know. Scholarships."

"I appreciate that. And I understand where you're coming from." Michael smiled again, and it was obvious he meant it. "Like I said, we're not here to question your coaching decisions."

"Thanks. I appreciate that."

"Your coaching methods differ from what the kids have been taught by Coach Kelly. That's not a bad thing. But to be fair to Coach Kelly we thought you should know more about her methods."

Michael paused for a moment and looked at his son. "Here in this small town, we're proud of her," he said. "She was born and raised here, then returned after all she accomplished in soccer on a national level."

"On a national level?" Cameron's dad looked surprised. "When we Googled her, we didn't see that, right?" James turned to Cameron, who nodded in agreement.

"There was nothing about that," said Cameron.

"She just got married about a month into the season," José added.

Cameron remembered Drew telling him that Coach Kelly helped her new husband on Saturday mornings.

"She changed her last name to Harrison," José continued. "If you want to learn about her background in the sport, you should Google 'Kelly Matthews, women's soccer.'"

Cameron pulled his smartphone from his pocket and swiped at the screen. He entered the search terms. The results were immediate.

"Dad," Cameron said after scanning the links. "This is pretty good stuff." Cameron handed his smartphone across to his Dad.

"Olympic-level playing," his Dad said, reading one of the headlines. "Top-ranked university player."

"It's not her style to talk about it," Michael said. "But she's the real deal. What you won't find on there are how many players from this small town she's coached who have gone on to get scholarships at major universities. Again, she doesn't talk about it, but most of us parents understand the reason she's so successful with our kids. And given what you've been doing with the kids during practice, you might find her approach very interesting."

"I'm listening," Cameron's dad said. "I'm open to anything that will help the kids get better at the game."

"We're headed out," Michael said. "How about you do some more research on Coach Kelly? Much better to find out for yourself and decide whether she's onto something."

CHAPTER 9

A NEW APPROACH

Cameron stood along the sideline at midfield. He held the ball above his head for a throw in. He couldn't help but think of his last game with his other team, the Royal Blues. They had been up 3–2 toward the end of the game. The smart choice then was to keep possession of the ball and run down the clock.

Now, however, the game was tied against the Bulls and their red jerseys. A goal would be huge either way. Take a chance for the win but risk losing?

Kyle Fenton, fast as usual, was breaking for an opening upfield. Trying a throw to him was the riskier play.

The safe throw was back down the field, to one of their own defensive players. But that would burn precious time off the clock, trying to advance the ball.

"Go for it, Cam!" His dad's voice came from the stands. "Have some fun."

What a difference watching the Coach Kelly videos had made for Cameron and his dad. For a while, Cameron had been planning on telling his dad that he had lost his love for the sport. It wasn't fun always stressing about making the right decision or who was watching that might give him a scholarship.

But the Coach Kelly videos they had watched together changed everything. Because she'd been an Olympic-level player, his dad had been open to learning from her approach.

The weakness of a team-first work ethic is that it takes away enthusiasm and creativity and doesn't give kids a chance to develop their natural talents. This was from the YouTube video of Coach Kelly Matthews explaining her philosophy. It had nearly a million views, and thousands of "thumbs-up" comments.

At a certain age when they are developing, let's not worry about winning. Let them enjoy some selfishness to get excited about what they can do with a ball. We can bring in teamwork and discipline later. But if they've lost their enthusiasm or don't have skills, no amount of teamwork is going to help them get to a college level of play.

After watching all the videos, his dad had agreed with Coach Kelly. Give full effort and don't worry if you make a mistake. What you learn from your mistakes will make you a better player. It may also help get that college scholarship.

Cameron flung the ball to where Kyle was breaking. It was a perfect throw. Kyle didn't have to break stride as he reached the ball.

Cameron didn't just stand and watch, though. He sprinted for an open space just behind Kyle. He hoped the ball would come back to him for an opportunity to score.

Still, if Kyle tried to hold on, no worries.

Yes. Soccer was fun for Cameron again. His dad had even stopped taking videos of the games. Now the family watched movies at night instead of replaying and analyzing soccer games.

With the crowd roaring, Cameron didn't yell for the ball. It came to him anyway.

He trapped it with his right foot. He knew he had about a second before a Bull forward was on him.

Cameron pretended to mishandle the ball to give the attacking player confidence. It was something he'd perfected during scrimmages in practice, against his own players.

It worked! The Bull player darted in close, hoping to strip him of the ball for a clear break down the field. Now the Bull player was badly out of position, with no way to turn back in time.

Cameron flipped the ball past the red-jersey player and caught up to it two steps later. The risk had paid off. Now they had a two-man advantage going toward the net.

Cameron kept dribbling forward. Another opponent peeled off to intercept him.

It was all Cameron needed.

Two of his teammates were rushing for open positions upfield. Better yet, one of them was José Padilla, who was a great shooter.

Time for a winning pass, Cameron thought. Not the safe, short pass. Not enough time in the game.

Cameron knew the attempt would catch the other team by surprise. All through the game he had been dumping the ball off immediately with short, safe passes. Not once had he shown the ability to bomb the ball.

He kept his head down, trying to fool them into thinking he hadn't seen the two Blazers cut past their midfielders.

Then the lightning strike.

Perfect pass to José. Perfect result.

José sent the ball past the goalie into the upper right corner of the net.

Game winner!

AUTHOR BIO

With over four million books in print, Sigmund Brouwer is a best-selling author of both children's and adult books. He lives in Red Deer, Alberta, Canada. For information about his school presentations, visit www.rockandroll-literacy.com.

ILLUSTRATOR BIO

Katie Wood fell in love with drawing when she was very young. Since graduating from Loughborough University School of Art and Design in 2004, she has been living her dream working as a freelance illustrator. From her studio in Leicester, England, she creates bright and lively illustrations for books and magazines all over the world.

GLOSSARY

aggressive (uh-GRES-iv)—forceful or assertive

creativity (kree-ay-TIV-ih-tee)—the ability to invent or create original or imaginative work

disadvantage (diss-uhd-VAN-tij)—an unfavorable circumstance

discipline (DISS-uh-plin)—control or determination brought about by training or self-control

emotion (i-MOH-shuhn)—a strong feeling or response such as joy, sadness, or love

enthusiasm (en-THOO-zee-az-uhm)—strong interest or excitement

faked (FAYKD)—to pretend to make a certain move in sports to fool the opponent

intercept (in-tur-SEPT)—to interrupt the movement of a player or pass, or to take control of the opponent's ball

percentage (pur-SEN-tij)—portion of a whole based on a total of one hundred parts

perspective (pur-SPEK-tiv)—a visual or mental view

possession (puh-ZESH-uhn)—ownership

successful (suhk-SESS-fuhl)—having brought about the result that was desired

DISCUSSION QUESTIONS

1. Why didn't Cameron enjoy playing soccer anymore? What was his reason for continuing to play even though he was no long having any fun?

2. Have you ever been in a sports situation where you've felt pressure? Was it pressure you put on yourself? Was it pressure from other people? Was it both? What do you think is the best way to deal with this pressure?

3. Why was Cameron so happy to be playing soccer again? Do you think you learn better when you are allowed to make mistakes? What do you see as a positive aspect of making mistakes?

WRITING PROMPTS

1. In Chapter 4, Cameron passes to Kyle but doesn't get a return pass when he is able to score. As a result, Kyle's decision cost Cameron's team a goal. Later in the game, the same situation occurs. This time, Cameron has a chance not to give the ball to Kyle but decides on the same smart choice and makes the pass. Once again, Kyle hogs the ball. Write a paragraph on whether you would have made that second pass, including your reasons.

2. In Chapter 7, Cameron's dad pulls José Padilla from the game because José held on to the ball instead of passing it like the players had been practicing. Cameron's dad was taking the opposite approach of Coach Kelly. Write a paragraph from José's point of view on how he felt for being punished by choosing one coach's approach over the other.

SOCCER GLOSSARY

Soccer has some great words to describe players, the field, and plays. Here are some terms to help you enjoy the game!

dribble—using your feet to move the ball with you, especially around an opponent

forward—one of the five offensive players on the team who try to advance the ball and score

goal—an area where a team scores against another team

goalkeeper—a player (also called a goalie or keeper) whose job is to defend the goal

head—to strike the ball with your forehead, either for a block, pass, or a shot at goal

mark—to guard an opposing player

midfield—the central area of the field between both goals

premier league—an association of teams that is first in importance or rank

pylon—a plastic traffic cone

referee—the sport official in charge of the game and ensuring that all the rules are followed

scrimmage—an informal or practice game, usually played to prepare for an actual match

sidelines—the area outside of the main field of play

winger—a midfield player on the left or right side of the field whose main job is to score goals

zone coverage—a type of defense where players are assigned a position instead of guarding another player

THE FUN DOESN'T STOP HERE!